This Book
BELONGS To:

PRINCESS PENELOPE

by Todd Mack   illustrated by Julia Gran

scholastic press ♛ new york

Text copyright © 2003 by Todd Mack. • Illustrations copyright © 2003 by Julia Gran • All rights reserved. Published by Scholastic Press, an imprint of Scholastic Inc., Publishers since 1920. • SCHOLASTIC, SCHOLASTIC PRESS, and associated logos are trademarks and/or registered trademarks of Scholastic Inc. • No part of this publication may be reproduced, stored in a retrieval system, or transmitted in any form or by any means, electronic, mechanical, photocopying, recording, or otherwise, without written permission of the publisher. For information regarding permission, write to Scholastic Inc., Attention: Permissions Department, 557 Broadway, New York, NY 10012. • LIBRARY OF CONGRESS CATALOGING-IN-PUBLICATION DATA Mack, Todd. Princess Penelope / by Todd Mack; illustrated by Julia Gran—1st ed. • p. cm. • Summary: Penelope is certain that she is royalty because of all the similarities between her life and that of a princess. • ISBN-13: 978-0-439-22436-9 • ISBN-10: 0-439-22436-5 (hardcover : alk. paper) [1. Parent and child—Fiction 2. Princesses—Fiction] I. Gran, Julia, ill. II. Title. PZ7.M18993 Pr 2003 E]—dc21 2002003080 10 9 8 7 08 09 10 11 12 • Printed in Singapore 46 • First edition, March 2003 • The text type was set in 35-point Refreshment Stand. The display type was set in Chicken King • The artwork was created using watercolors. • Book design by Marijka Kostiw

To Caroline,
for the inspiration
–T. M.

To Michael
– J. G.

PENELOPE was a princess.
She was absolutely certain.

She read lots of fairy tales,
so she was an
EXPERT on princesses.

Her grandmother even gave her a princess crown.
"This is just like the crown I used to wear when
I was a girl," she told Penelope.

Every morning, Penelope was awoken by a kiss from the king and the queen.
"GOOD MORNING, MY LITTLE PRINCESS!" the queen always reveled.

"I'M PENELOPE,
AND I AM A PRINCESS!"
she sang at the top of her lungs.
The king and the queen
had to share a room and a bed,
but Penelope had her very own bed
in her very own room,
JUST LIKE A PRINCESS.

Princesses had chambermaids
who buttoned and zipped them.
So did Penelope.

Princesses changed their outfits
many times a day.
Penelope LOVED to change
her outfits.

"I'M PENELOPE, AND I AM A PRINCESS!" she cheered as she pranced through the palace.

Princesses sat
on thrones.
Penelope had
LOTS
of thrones.

"I'M PENELOPE, AND I AM A PRINCESS,"

she announced at her midday meal.

Princesses ate FANCY foods,
served on SPECIAL dishes.
They had servants who waited on them
hand and foot. So did Penelope.

The servants cleaned up after their princess and comforted her in times of need.

"I'M PENELOPE, AND I AM A PRINCESS,"
she caroled when she strolled through her kingdom.
Princesses rode in chariots. Penelope had LOTS of chariots.
Princesses were famous. Penelope was famous.

Everywhere she went, people stopped and waved.

They smiled and threw kisses.

Many of them she'd never met before.

They ALL told her she was beautiful.

Princesses made rules.

PENELOPE made rules.

The king said she ruled the roost.

Princesses liked to give commands and make demands.

PENELOPE liked to give commands and make demands.

Sometimes she had to sit on one of her thrones
after making too many demands.

"I'M PENELOPE, AND I AM A PRINCESS,"
she chanted while the queen drew her bath.
Every night, Penelope was pampered, just like a princess.

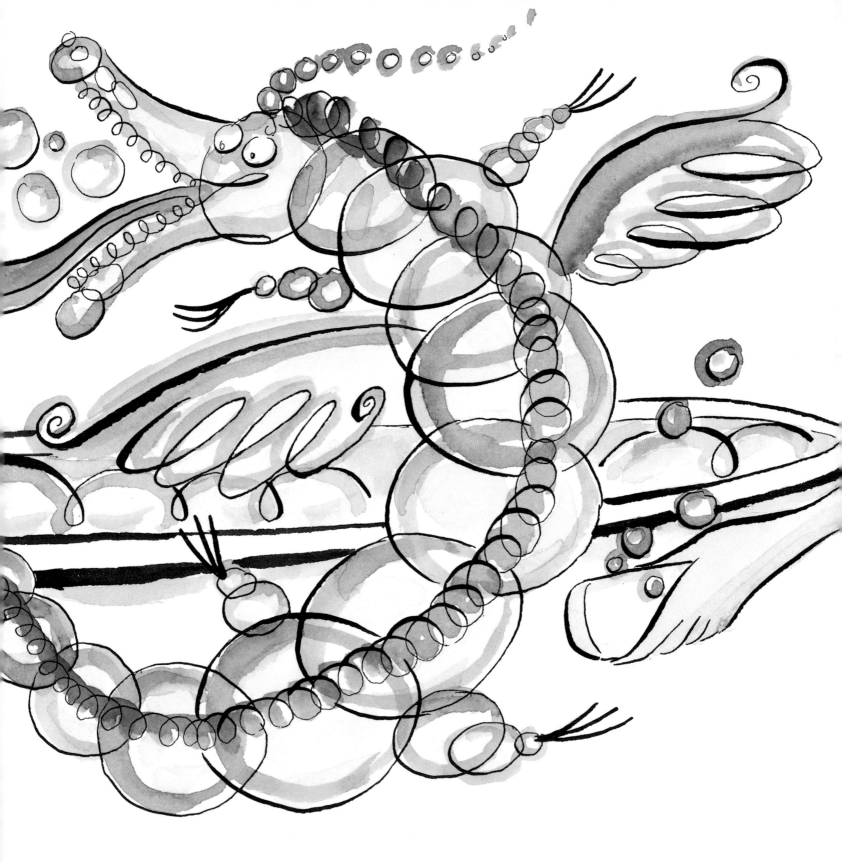

Then she put on a royal robe and climbed into bed.
The king read her favorite fairy tale before he
and the queen kissed Penelope good night.
"SWEET DREAMS, MY LITTLE PRINCESS,"
the king always whispered.

Penelope was a princess.
She was absolutely certain.